This Little Tiger book belongs to:

_____

_____

_____

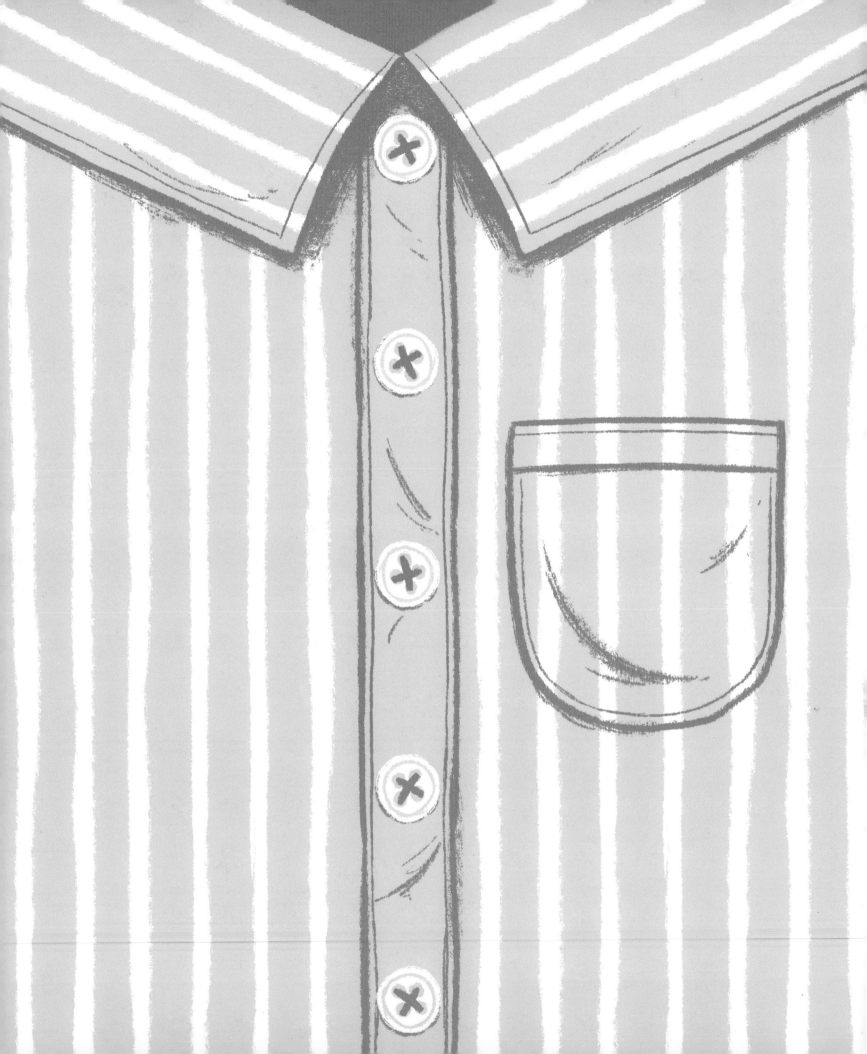

There's a Bison BOUNCING on the Bed!

Paul Bright

Chris Chatterton

BOUNCING
FOR
DUMMIES

BOUNCE LIKE
THE BEST

LITTLE TIGER PRESS
London

Big, brown bison is bouncing on the bed.

The bed starts to "BEND."

The bed starts to "SHAKE."

I really hope the bed won't

BREAK!

Aardvark says,
"That looks like fun.
I think there's room
for more than one!"

Chipmunk says,
"I'll jump with you.
I'm sure there's room
for more than two!"

Then Beetle says,
"Make way for me!
There must be room
for more than three!"

Oh, what a
thump
and
bump
they make.
I really hope
the bed
won't . . .

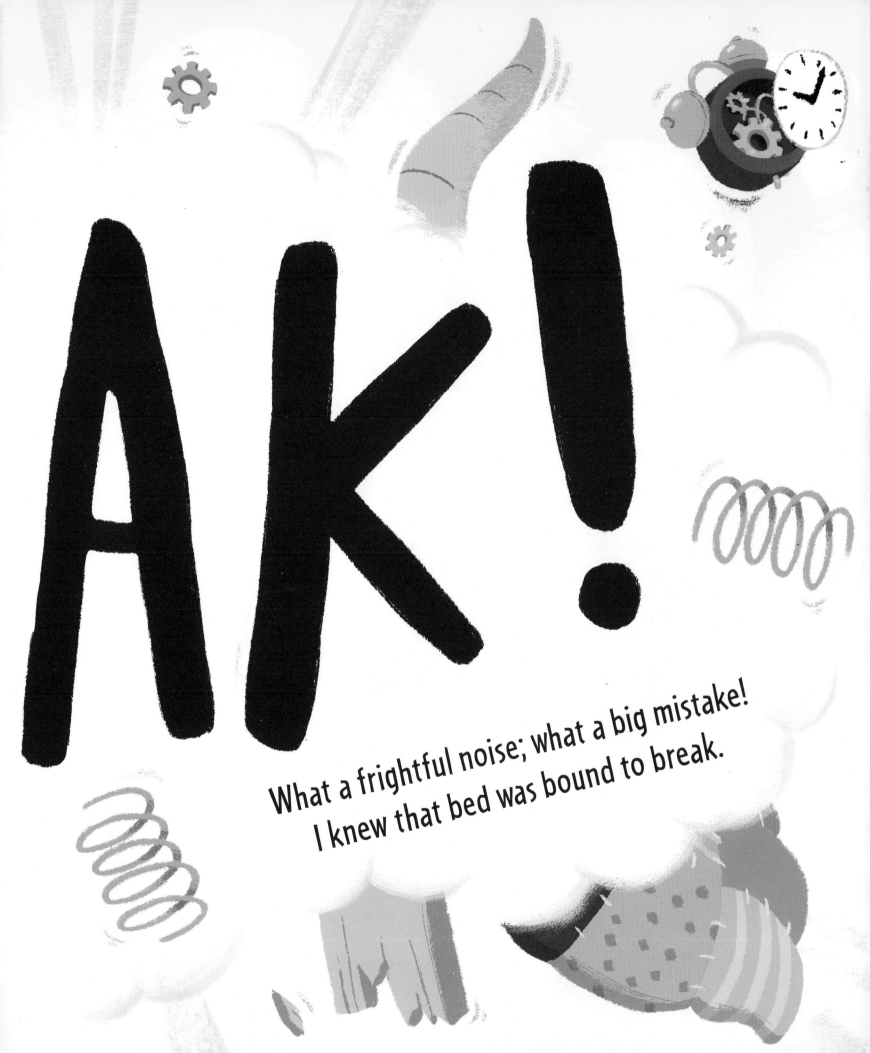

AK!

What a frightful noise; what a big mistake!
I knew that bed was bound to break.

Bison says,
"Look what you've done!
It was all right with only one!"

Aardvark says,
"It must be you!
It didn't break when there
were two."

Chipmunk says,
"It wasn't me!
The bed was strong enough
for three."

"Stop!"

shouts beetle.

"It's still shaking!
Yes it is – the bed's still quaking!
Can't you see – there's no mistaking –
Something in the bed is waking!"

Grizzly Bear - for that's his name -
Wakes up and says,

"You're all to blame!
You've all been bouncing on my bed,
And on my tummy and my head!"

"Now find a hammer,
nails and glue,
And make my bed
as good as new."

They fix and mend until it's done.

"NOW,"

growls Bear,
"it's time for . . ."

FUN!

For I and J, the best bed-bouncers in the world

~ P B

For Hilda & Cyril

~ C C

LITTLE TIGER PRESS
1 The Coda Centre, 189 Munster Road, London SW6 6AW
www.littletiger.co.uk

First published in Great Britain 2016
This edition published 2016

Text copyright © Paul Bright 2016
Illustrations copyright © Chris Chatterton 2016

A CIP catalogue record for this book is
available from the British Library

Printed in China · LTP/1800/1243/0815

2 4 6 8 10 9 7 5 3 1

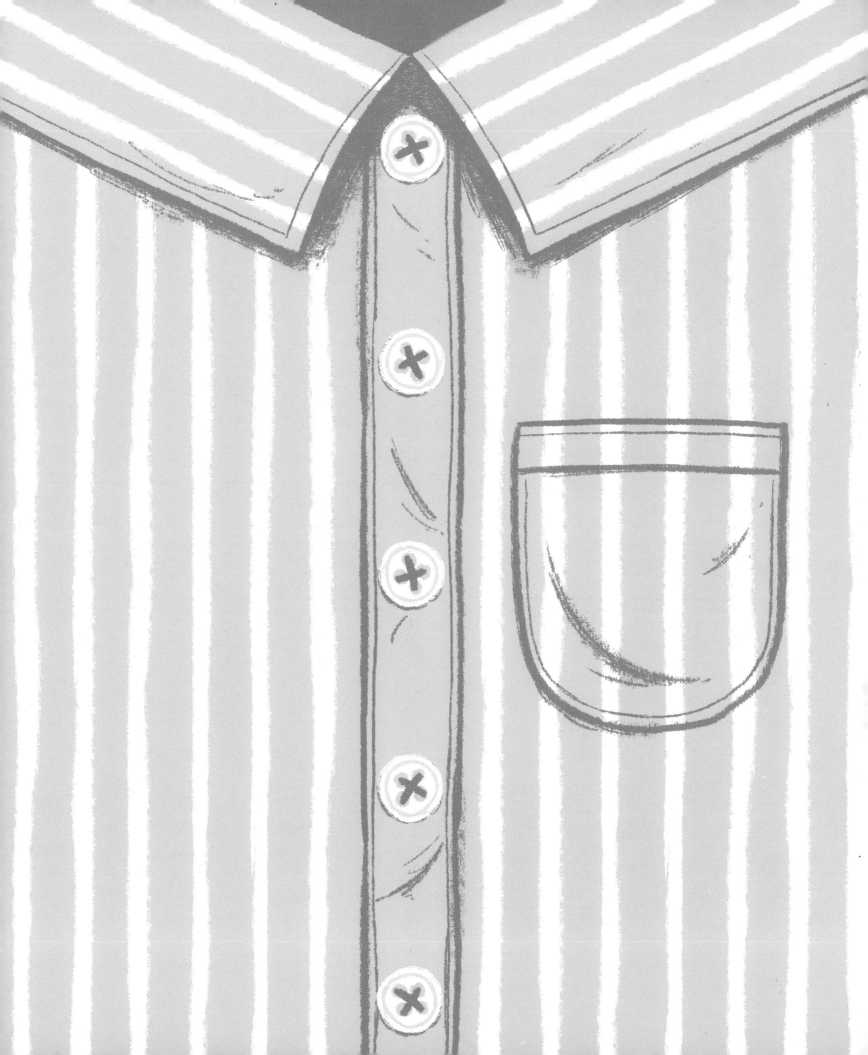

More brilliant books to read at bedtime from Little Tiger Press!

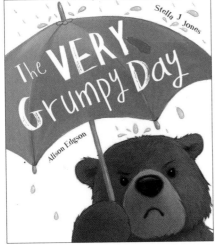

For information regarding any of the above titles
or for our catalogue, please contact us:
Little Tiger Press, 1 The Coda Centre,
189 Munster Road, London SW6 6AW
Tel: 020 7385 6333
E-mail: contact@littletiger.co.uk
www.littletiger.co.uk